Happy Ever After

ORCHARD BOOKS
338 Euston Road, London NW1 3BH
Orchard Books Australia
Level 17/207 Kent Street, Sydney, NSW 2000

First published in hardback in 2010 by Orchard Books
First published in paperback in 2011

ISBN 978 1 40830 752 6 (HB)
ISBN 978 1 40830 758 8 (PB)

A CIP catalogue record for this book is available from the British Library.

1 3 5 7 9 10 8 6 4 2 (HB)
1 3 5 7 9 10 8 6 4 2 (PB)

Printed in Great Britain

Orchard Books is a division of Hachette Children's Books,
an Hachette UK company.
www.hachette.co.uk

Tony Bradman

Happy Ever After

MR BEAR
GETS ALARMED

Illustrated by Sarah Warburton

ORCHARD BOOKS

"You're in a funny mood," said Mrs Bear, turning to her husband. "I hope you're not still brooding about what happened last week. You need to get over it, dear."

The Three Bears had just eaten a delicious
supper in their little cottage. Now Mr and
Mrs Bear were doing the washing up while
Baby Bear watched TV.

"Brooding? Me? Certainly not!" said Mr Bear.
"But I *have* been doing some thinking...

"I've decided we should get a burglar alarm."

"Isn't that a bit extreme?" said Mrs Bear, frowning. "Goldilocks won't do it again, I'm sure. Her parents gave her such a telling off when I took her home."

"Maybe she won't," said Mr Bear. "But if a young girl can break in, then anybody can. And the Forest is full of dangerous characters these days. You've seen the scary stories on the news."

The truth was that Mr Bear had been
very rattled by the whole Goldilocks incident.

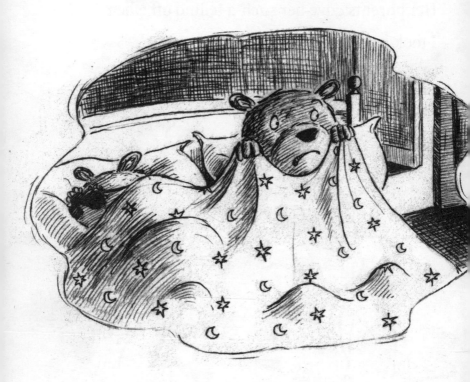

He hadn't slept well since then, and woke up
several times each night, convinced he could hear
a window being opened or footsteps on the
stairs... No, the only way to stop worrying was to
get alarmed, and the sooner the better.

"I don't take as much notice of the news
stories as you do," said Mrs Bear, shrugging.

"But you can have an alarm if it will make you
happy. Now, how about a cup of tea?"

But Mr Bear's cup of tea went cold. He
sat in front of his computer, searching the
Forest Web for companies that fitted alarms.
He hadn't realised there were so many! And the
alarm systems they sold were *so* complicated.

10

"You could try any of them," said Mrs Bear.
"They all look the same to me."

"But they're not," murmured Mr Bear.
"What if I choose one that's no good?"

"Fine, you carry on," said Mrs Bear.
"I'll put Baby Bear to bed on my own."

Mr Bear finally made his choice hours later, long after Baby Bear *and* Mrs Bear had gone to bed. And the sun had barely risen the next morning when the man from Wizard Security rang the doorbell.

Soon he was laying cables and wires everywhere. Mrs Bear was still in her nightdress, and not very happy about being disturbed so early.

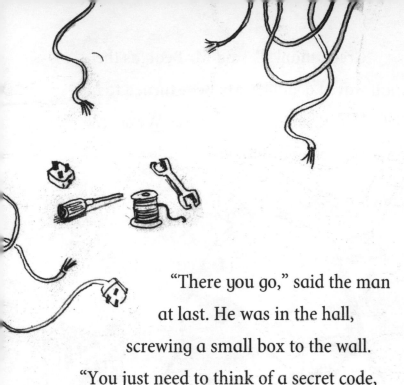

"There you go," said the man
at last. He was in the hall,
screwing a small box to the wall.
"You just need to think of a secret code,
then you're all set. You tap it into this keypad to
turn the system on and off."

"Great, thanks!" said Mr Bear, as the man waved goodbye. Mr Bear turned to his wife. "Now, let's think of a code. We should make it really hard to guess."

"I'll leave that up to you, dear," sighed Mrs Bear. "I have to get ready."

Mr Bear always gave Mrs Bear a lift
to work, then dropped Baby Bear off at school.
He wrote down the code he had made up and
gave it to them.

They were supposed to memorise it,
then destroy the pieces of paper.

Mr Bear drove home in the sunshine, feeling happy and relaxed for the first time in ages.

He tapped in the code to turn off the alarm, then cleared away the breakfast dishes.

He made the beds and did some ironing –
one of his favourite things.

That night he slept really well.

Life went by peacefully, and on Saturday
they went shopping to buy Baby Bear
some school shoes. Back at home, Mr Bear
was locking the car when he gasped in horror
at his wife.

Mrs Bear was reading their secret code *from a piece of paper*!

"What are you doing?" said Mr Bear.
"You were supposed to destroy that!"

"Well, you made the code too hard to remember, so I didn't," said Mrs Bear. "I don't see what the big deal is, anyway. I keep it in my handbag."

"But…but what if someone steals your handbag?" squeaked Mr Bear.

"No problem," Baby Bear piped up. "I've written the code on my paw."

"Oh no!" groaned Mr Bear. "What if someone has seen it already? We'll have to change it. Maybe we should have a different code every week, or even for every day."

Mrs Bear and Baby Bear rolled their eyes, but Mr Bear made them promise they would memorise the new code.

But soon Mr Bear decided that it still wasn't enough. So he called Wizard Security once more…

"There you go," said the man. "Now you've got the best system money can buy. Separate alarms in each room…

…cameras inside the cottage…

…and in the garden…

…and a panic button that connects you directly to the Forest Police."

Mr Bear relaxed again. But that night, just after the Three Bears had gone to bed, there was a terrible noise.

DANG-A-LANG
-A-LANG!

All the alarms had gone off at once!

Mrs Bear grabbed Baby Bear, Mr Bear ran
round yelling, and the Forest Police arrived,
lights flashing and sirens wailing.

WHOOP-WHOOP-WHOOP!

"You can calm down now, Mr Bear,"
said a policeman, once the alarms had stopped.
"We're pretty sure no one was trying to break in.
These complicated alarm systems can sometimes
be too sensitive. A squirrel might have set it off,
or even a mouse."

"Oh, terrific," muttered Mrs Bear.
Then she took Baby Bear back to bed.

After that, the Three Bears were *very* careful at night. But hardly a day went by without one of the alarms going off…

…and sometimes all of them at once.

The Three Bears got to know the Forest Police rather well.

Then one day, much to Mr Bear's surprise, the alarms *didn't* go off. They didn't go off the next day, either. Mr Bear was very pleased.

"You see?" he said, grinning. "I knew they would settle down eventually."

"Of course you did, dear," said Mrs Bear. For some reason, Baby Bear giggled, and Mrs Bear frowned at him. "Now, what shall we have for tea?"

It was a happy and relaxed Mr Bear who went to bed that evening.

He fell into a deep, dreamless sleep…
but suddenly he was awake, his heart pounding.

He could hear footsteps on the stairs – and
he couldn't hear any alarms!

Mr Bear crept out of the bedroom and
onto the landing. He looked down, and there
was Mrs Bear in the hall, tapping a code
into the keypad.

She glanced up at him, and a
guilty expression passed over her face.
Then she scowled.

"All right, you've caught me," she said, and sighed. "We've been turning the alarms off every night. We just couldn't cope with it any more."

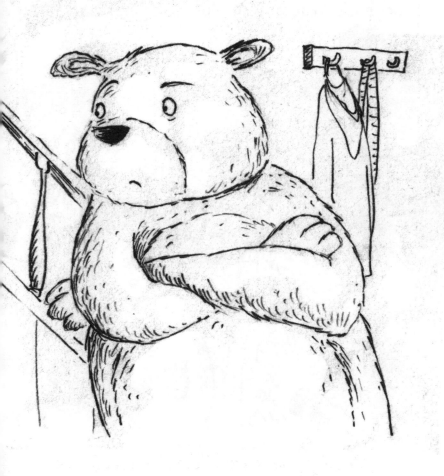

"Oh no! What if someone had broken in?"
moaned Mr Bear. "What if…"

"They didn't though, did they?" said
Mrs Bear. "And what if you're just worrying
too much? What if your alarms are making
our lives a misery?"

Mr Bear realised Mrs Bear was right.
Now it was his turn to feel guilty.

The alarms certainly hadn't stopped him
worrying, had they? In fact they had only
made things much worse.

Mr Bear did a lot of thinking that day, and finally he came to a decision.

He called Wizard Security for the last time, and it wasn't long before all the alarms were gone.

The next morning, Mr Bear woke up in a cheerful mood.

"What a lovely day!" he said. "Let's go for a walk."

They set off on their usual path through the Forest. Baby Bear skipped ahead of his parents.

Suddenly Mrs Bear stopped and looked at
her husband.

"Oh no, I forgot to lock the front door!" she said. "We'd better go back!"

Mr Bear turned to her, and for an instant he felt a little panicky…

But then he smiled and shrugged, and
took her arm.

"Not to worry," he said as they walked on.
"I'm sure it will be all right."

And so the Three Bears lived quietly and calmly but most of all…

…*HAPPILY EVER AFTER!*